CUENTO DE LUZ

For you, Mom, because when I was little you showed me all your dresses,
and among them, I learned to live.

- Mónica Carretero -

Mom's Dresses

Text & illustrations © 2016 Mónica Carretero
This edition © 2016 Cuento de Luz SL
Calle Claveles, 10 | Urb. Monteclaro | Pozuelo de Alarcón | 28223 | Madrid | Spain
www.cuentodeluz.com
Title in Spanish: Los vestidos de mamá
English translation by Jon Brokenbrow

ISBN: 978-84-16147-74-8

Printed by Shanghai Chenxi Printing Co., Ltd. January 2016, print number 1546-4

FSC
www.fsc.org
MIX
Paper from responsible sources
FSC® C007923

Mom's Dresses

Mónica Carretero

Sometimes, Mom wears a checkered dress.

Then I'm a princess on horseback, who's rescued a pawn.

Other times, she wears a dress with houses.

And I'm a giant walking through the streets, taking great big steps.

What a beautiful sunny day! Mom's dressed in blue! And off I sail in my ship. There are seagulls in the air, and mermaids in the sea.

Today, Mom's wearing a dress with a thousand flowers, and I run amongst them, decorating my hair with all of their colors.

Whenever Mom wears her stripy dress . . .

I start to sing with
the notes, jumping
between the lines
as I hum along.

Yesterday, Mom wore a dress covered in cupcakes, so I organized a very special tea party.

The guests wore all their finest
clothes, top hats, neckties, ribbons,
and bows.

One day when Mom was sad, she wore a black dress.
I picked up my flashlight, and hugged her in silence.

Today, Mom woke up with hearts on her nightgown.

I can feel a tingling, and I can't stop blushing. Someone's cast a spell on me, and there's a buzzing in my head.

If Mom wears a dress with squares,
I pick up a pencil and write my
favorite words . . .

bird

balloon

sun

ma

cloud

y

tatoes

sock

ponytails

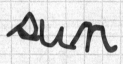

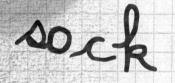

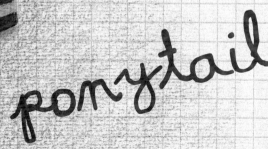

When Mom wears her white dress . . .
it makes me feel inspired.

So I pick up my brushes,
and paint.

I love it when Mom wears her
dress with the birds . . .
so I can fly high up in the sky,
over the hills and far away.

Tonight she's wearing
the dress that's
covered in stars.
I cuddle into her
arms, and we fall fast
asleep together.

Here are some
cutouts for you
to color in! You can
dress up the little girl
from the story however
you like! Each of the pictures
is reversible: one side is already
decorated, but you can have fun
decorating the other side yourself and
have a reversible piece of clothing. Before
you start, cut out the picture of the little girl
and stick her onto a piece of cardboard. Then
fold back the tab under her feet so that she stays
upright. You could also try creating some totally new
dresses! Have fun playing with your own creations!

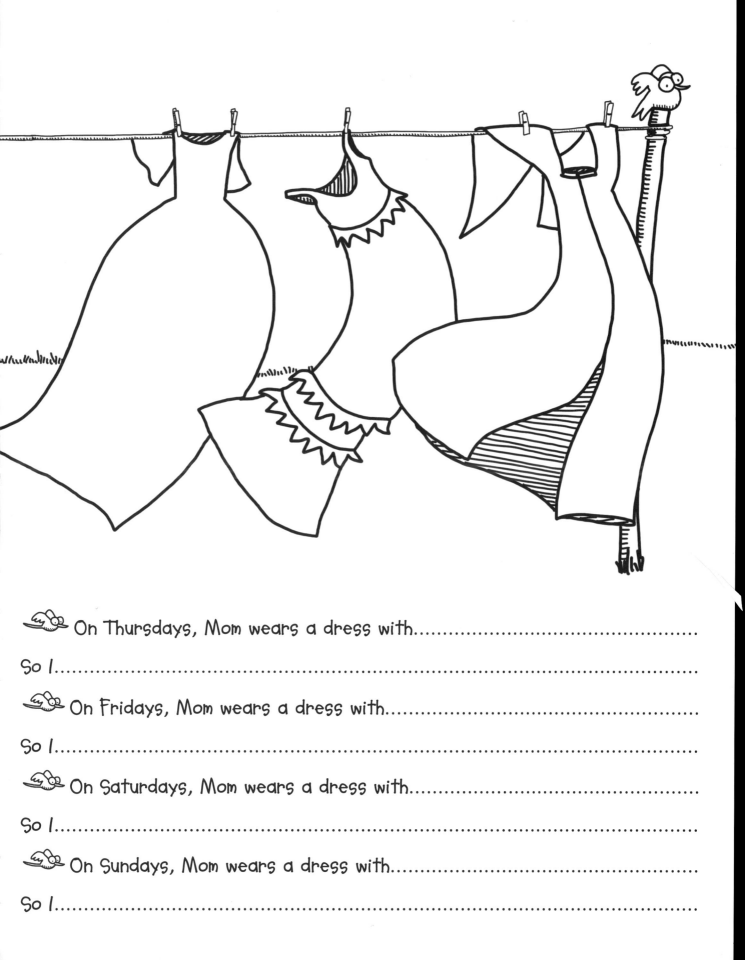

On Thursdays, Mom wears a dress with..

So I..

On Fridays, Mom wears a dress with..

So I..

On Saturdays, Mom wears a dress with...

So I..

On Sundays, Mom wears a dress with...

So I..